My dearest puppy, Storm,

I hope this letter reaches you safe and sound. You have been so brave since you had to flee from the evil wolf Shadow.

Do not worry about me. I will hide here until you are strong enough to return and lead our pack. For now you must move on – you must hide from Shadow and his spies. If Shadow finds this letter I believe he will try to destroy it . . .

Find a good friend – someone to help finish my message to you. Because what I have to say to you is important. What I have to say is this: you must always

Please don't feel lonely. Trust in your friends and all will be well.

Your loving mother,

Canista

Sue Bentley's books for children often include animals, fairies and wildlife. She lives in Northampton and enjoys reading, going to the cinema, relaxing by her garden pond and watching the birds feeding their babies on the lawn. At school she was always getting told off for daydreaming or staring out of the window – but she now realizes that she was storing up ideas for when she became a writer. She has met and owned many cats and dogs and each one has brought a special kind of magic to her life.

Sue Bentley

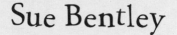

Star of the Show

Illustrated by Angela Swan

PUFFIN

To Butch – a boisterous playmate

with a mind of his own

PUFFIN BOOKS

Published by the Penguin Group
Penguin Books Ltd, 80 Strand, London WC2R ORL, England
Penguin Group (USA) Inc., 375 Hudson Street, New York, New York 10014, USA
Penguin Group (Canada), 90 Eglinton Avenue East, Suite 700, Toronto, Ontario, Canada M4P 2Y3
(a division of Pearson Penguin Canada Inc.)
Penguin Ireland, 25 St Stephen's Green, Dublin 2, Ireland (a division of Penguin Books Ltd)
Penguin Group (Australia), 250 Camberwell Road, Camberwell, Victoria 3124, Australia
(a division of Pearson Australia Group Pty Ltd)
Penguin Books India Pvt Ltd, 11 Community Centre, Panchsheel Park, New Delhi – 110 017, India
Penguin Group (NZ), 67 Apollo Drive, Rosedale, North Shore 0632, New Zealand
(a division of Pearson New Zealand Ltd)
Penguin Books (South Africa) (Pty) Ltd, 24 Sturdee Avenue, Rosebank,
Johannesburg 2196, South Africa

Penguin Books Ltd, Registered Offices: 80 Strand, London WC2R ORL, England

puffinbooks.com

First published 2008
7

Text copyright © Sue Bentley, 2008
Illustrations copyright © Angela Swan, 2008
All rights reserved

The moral right of the author and illustrator has been asserted

Set in Bembo
Typeset by Palimpsest Book Production Limited,
Grangemouth, Stirlingshire
Made and printed in England by Clays Ltd, St Ives plc

British Library Cataloguing in Publication Data
A CIP catalogue record for this book is available from the British Library

ISBN: 978-0-141-32353-4

www.greenpenguin.co.uk

Penguin Books is committed to a sustainable future
for our business, our readers and our planet.
The book in your hands is made from paper
certified by the Forest Stewardship Council.

Prologue

The young silver-grey wolf froze as a
terrifying howl rose into the air.

'Shadow!' Storm gasped. The big,
fierce lone wolf, who had attacked
Storm's pack and left his mother
wounded, was very close.

Suddenly a dazzling flash of bright
golden light and a shower of sparks
filled the air. Where the young wolf had

stood there now crouched a tiny rusty-coloured spaniel puppy with wavy fur, long floppy ears and midnight-blue eyes.

Storm's puppy heart beat fast as he bounded forward across the snow. He looked from left to right, trying to find a hiding place, but the flat plain stretched in all directions like a white desert.

He saw a tiny speck in the distance, which was growing bigger as it came closer. It was an adult wolf.

Storm whimpered with terror.

His wobbly legs collapsed beneath him and Storm felt himself sinking. Chunks of snow rained on to the little puppy as he sank down into an ice cave. He lay there trembling, hoping that his hiding place would protect him.

Moments later, Storm heard paws scrabbling above him as a large animal enlarged the entrance to the cave. This was it. Shadow had dug him out!

A wolf's head appeared, framed by the night sky. 'Are you hurt, my son?' growled a soft velvety voice.

'Mother!' Storm woofed in relief, wagging his little tail. 'I am fine now!'

Canista slid right in and crouched beside her disguised cub. She licked his muzzle in greeting. 'I am glad to see you again, but it is not yet safe for you to return. Shadow is very close. He wants to lead the Moon-claw pack, but they will not follow him while you live.'

Storm's midnight-blue eyes sparked

with fear and anger. 'Perhaps we should face him and fight him!'

Canista showed her sharp white teeth in a proud smile. 'Bravely said, Storm. But Shadow is too strong for you to face alone. And I am still too weak from his poisonous bite to help you. Use this disguise. Go to the other world and return when you are stronger.' She winced and her eyes clouded with pain.

Storm huffed out a warm glittering puppy breath. It shimmered around Canista's wounded leg in a golden mist and then sank into her grey fur. 'Thank you. The pain is fading,' she rumbled softly.

Suddenly, another fierce howl seemed to tear at the icy air.

'Shadow is coming! Save yourself. Go . . .' Canista urged.

Bright gold sparks ignited in the tiny puppy's wavy reddish-brown fur. Storm whined as he felt the power building within him. The golden light around him grew brighter. And brighter . . .

Chapter
ONE

Tessa Churchill's tummy lurched with
excitement as she saw all the huge
trucks and trailers in front of Harpford
Manor. There were lights and
equipment everywhere and lots of
people pushing trolleys and racks of
costumes.

'I still can't believe that I'm going to
be in *Timepiece* with Donny Jenton. I'm

so nervous,' Tessa said to her mum.

'That's not surprising. This is your
first part in a film,' Mrs Churchill said,
giving her a hug. 'Come on, let's go
and find Judith Raunds, the lady who'll
be looking after you.'

Tessa nodded as she and her mum
began walking towards the main house.

She was also looking forward to meeting the other two girls who had parts in the film – Tessa had been excited to hear that they were about the same age as her. It would be great to hang out with new friends while she was here.

A woman came out of a side door and greeted them both. 'Hello, Mrs Churchill, I'm Judith. And this must be Tessa. I'm delighted to meet you.' She had a light-brown pony tail and a pleasant round face and was wearing a blue T-shirt, jeans and trainers.

Mrs Churchill shook Judith's hand. 'Hello, Judith. It's nice to put a face to the voice. And thanks for being so understanding when I phoned to say we'd be late arriving,' she said.

Judith smiled. 'No problem. Hold-ups at airports are a fact of life these days.' She turned to Tessa. 'Let's go inside. Kelly and Fay arrived earlier. They're having supper. I'll introduce you.'

'OK.' Tessa smiled at Judith who seemed really nice. She felt herself starting to relax. She turned to her mum. 'I'll be fine now. You don't have to stay with me.'

'Sure? All right then, darling. I'll get going.' Mrs Churchill kissed her daughter on the cheek. 'See you next week. And don't forget to phone.'

'You bet! Give my love to Dad when you get back to the yacht. Bye!' Tessa said. She waited until her mum drove off and then followed Judith into the house.

They went through a maze of
corridors until they reached a very
grand room. It had panelling on the
walls and a high domed ceiling,
which was painted with clouds and
cherubs. Expensive-looking paintings of
rather stern people were hung all
around.

A self-service counter with hot and
cold food had been set up along one
wall and there were neat rows of tables
and chairs. The room buzzed with
voices and laughter.

'This is where you'll have all your
meals. Catering is 24/7, so you can
get a hot drink or food whenever you
want it,' Judith explained. She led Tessa
over to two girls who were sitting at a
table by themselves. 'These are your

young co-stars, Kelly Lucas and Fay Hinson. Kelly, Fay, this is Tessa Churchill.'

'Hi,' Tessa said, smiling.

Fay and Kelly smiled back.

'I'll leave you all to get to know one another. I've got a few things to do, so I'll pop back in a bit and see if you need anything,' Judith said to Tessa.

'OK, thanks,' Tessa said, smiling
at the two girls as Judith moved
away.

Kelly's friendly expression suddenly
changed. 'So you're the kid with
posh parents. I bet you loved keeping
everyone waiting, so you could get
all the attention when you *finally*
arrived!' She looked about twelve
years old, two years older than Tessa,
and had a thin face and short dark
hair.

Tessa felt herself going red. At her
first drama school, she'd been bullied
because of having rich parents, so
now she kept quiet about it. Kelly
must have listened to Judith on the
phone to her mum and heard about
the holiday on the family yacht, which

Tessa was cutting short to work on this film.

Tessa took a breath to calm her nerves before answering, 'Let's get something straight, Kelly. Acting is all that matters to me and I just want to do my best, the same as you. So leave my mum and dad out of it. OK?' she said.

Kelly looked surprised and even a tiny bit impressed. She seemed about to say something else and then she shrugged. 'Whatever,' she said, getting up and wandering over to the service counter.

Tessa looked at Fay, hoping that the other girl might be easier to get on with. 'Which stage school do you come from?' she asked her.

'Ashton School of Drama,' Fay murmured without looking up. She was stirring her plate of pasta around with a fork and seemed to be in a world of her own.

Tessa tried again. 'Have you seen Donny Jenton yet?'

'No. Someone said they'd seen his

little pug dog, Lady. So he's here. But there's masses of security around him. We'll probably only get to meet Donny when we're acting in a scene with him,' Fay said gloomily. She pushed her plate away and drooped forward to rest her chin on her elbows.

Tessa felt her spirits sinking. Fay definitely didn't seem any more bothered than Kelly about making friends with her.

A wave of loneliness rose in Tessa as she wished that she'd asked her mum to stay for a bit longer. But she squared her shoulders and resolved to make the best of it.

Tessa decided to go straight up to her room and start unpacking. She didn't feel much like eating and there didn't

seem much point in sitting here with
Fay and Kelly.

Tessa rose to her feet. 'How do I get
to our room?' she asked Fay.

Fay looked up at last. She had
freckled skin and hazel eyes and
would have been pretty if her face
hadn't been screwed into a frown. 'Um
. . . through that door, up two lots of
stairs and turn left. It's the third room
you come to.'

'Thanks.' As Tessa went out, she passed
Kelly who was on her way back to the
table with a glass of Coke. 'Too good to
sit and eat with us, are you, Princess?'
the older girl mocked.

Tessa ignored her, but to her
annoyance she felt a lump rising in her
throat as she remembered what it was

like to be bullied. Well, she wasn't a
scared little kid any more. She was ten
years old and had been in heaps of TV
adverts and theatre plays and she was
determined not to cry.

Bolting up the stairs two at a time,
Tessa found their room easily. She saw
that her suitcase had been brought up

and left on the rug. She looked around. The two beds on either side of the window had been taken. The only one left was in a gloomy alcove. There was barely room for the bed, a small bedside cabinet and a battered-looking wardrobe.

'This just gets better!' Tessa grumbled, picking up her case and dumping it on her bed. She opened her case, grabbed a bundle of clothes at random and opened the wardrobe. The door swung wide with a loud, rusty squeak and Tessa was blinded by a dazzling bright gold flash.

'Oh!' Tessa gasped, staggering back. When she could see again, Tessa saw a tiny puppy with wavy reddish-brown fur, floppy ears and bright midnight-blue eyes looking up at her from the bottom of the wardrobe.

'Can you help me, please?' it woofed.

Chapter
TWO

Tessa stared down at the tiny puppy in complete surprise, wondering where it had come from. The wardrobe door squeaking open had made it sound like the puppy had spoken! Tessa shook her head at the silly idea.

'What are you doing in there?' she crooned, bending over to look more closely at the puppy. 'Aren't you cute? You look like a little spaniel.'

'I have arrived here from far away.
I am Storm of the Moon-claw pack.
Who are you?' the puppy woofed.

Tessa's eyes widened in shock and the
pile of clothes slipped from her numb
fingers and crumpled to the floor. 'You
really c-can talk,' she gasped in
amazement.

The puppy nodded, looking up at her with large, intelligent blue eyes, as if waiting for her to reply to its question. Although it was only tiny, it didn't seem to be very afraid of her.

'I'm . . . um . . . Tessa Churchill. I'm an actress. I'm here to make a film.'

The puppy dipped its tiny head in a formal bow. 'I am honoured to meet you, Tessa. I must hide. Can you help me?' he said in a gruff little bark.

'Is someone after you?' Tessa asked. She still couldn't quite believe that this was happening, but her curiosity was beginning to get the better of her shock.

Storm's big dewy eyes sparked with anger and fear. 'Shadow, the evil lone wolf is looking for me. He has killed my father and three litter brothers and wounded my mother. He wants to lead the Moon-claw pack but the other wolves are waiting until I am strong enough to lead them.'

Tessa frowned. 'But how can you lead a wolf pack? You're just a pu—'

'I will show you! Please stand back,' Storm interrupted in a soft bark.

He leapt out of the wardrobe and stood on the carpet. There was another dazzling flash of bright gold light and sparks sprayed out, floating down around Tessa and crackling where they landed.

'Oh!' she gasped as the tiny puppy vanished and in its place there stood a muscular young silver-grey wolf. Tessa nervously eyed the wolf's large sharp teeth and powerful paws that seemed much too big for his body. 'Storm?'

'Yes, Tessa, it is me. Do not be afraid. I will not harm you,' Storm growled gently.

Before Tessa had time to get used to the majestic sight of Storm as a young wolf, there was a final bright burst of light and he reappeared in the room as a tiny puppy with wavy rusty-coloured fur and a swishy tail.

'That's an amazing disguise. No one would know that you're a wolf,' Tessa said, deeply impressed.

'Shadow will know if he finds me. I need to hide now,' Storm whined.

Tessa saw that he was starting to tremble all over. With his startling midnight-blue eyes, wet reddish-brown nose and little pointed face, Storm was the most adorable thing she had ever seen.

Her soft heart went out to the helpless little puppy who needed a friend as much as she did.

'I'll look after you. You can sleep here with me —' she began and then stopped as she realized that pets probably wouldn't be allowed. 'I could try and hide you, but I'm sharing this room with two other girls. Fay's all wrapped up in herself, so she might not notice. But I bet Kelly would love to snitch on me, just to get me into trouble!' she guessed.

Storm showed his little pointed teeth in a doggy grin. 'I would love to stay

here with you, Tessa. I will use my
magic so that only you will be able to
see and hear me.'

'You can make yourself invisible?
Cool! Then there's no problem. You can
stay in here and Kelly and Fay won't
know a thing.' Tessa bent down to pick
Storm up and stroke his soft little head.

'Thank you, Tessa!' Storm snuggled up
to her, wagging his little red-brown tail.

She was glad of her bed in the dim alcove now. It would be much easier to cuddle up with Storm and talk to him without attracting attention from her room-mates.

As Tessa put Storm down and then picked up her clothes to hang them away, the tiny puppy jumped on to her duvet. He gave a contented sigh and curled up for a nap.

Tessa smiled to herself in delight. This was better than any film and Kelly's and Fay's unfriendliness didn't matter any more. She wouldn't be lonely now that she had this amazing magic puppy for company.

Tessa woke early the following morning. She could feel a warm weight tucked into the crook of her arm. Feeling her stir, Storm sat up and stretched.

'Hello, Storm. Did you sleep OK?' Tessa whispered so that the other girls couldn't hear her.

'Very well. This is a good place,' Storm woofed.

The bedroom door opened and Judith popped her head in. 'Rise and shine, everyone!' she said brightly. 'Come down for breakfast as soon as you can, please. School lessons start in an hour.'

'OK. I'll be right there!' Tessa said.

Judith flashed a smile at her before going out and closing the door.

'It's a shame that our schools have to set work for us. I can't wait until I'm older and then I can act all day,' Tessa whispered to Storm.

Kelly jumped up, got straight out of bed and went to the bathroom, but Fay sat up blinking and rubbing her eyes sleepily.

Tessa wasn't surprised. Fay had been writing something in a big green book for ages before she went to sleep. It was there on top of her bedside cabinet.

'Is that your scrapbook?' Tessa asked Fay. She knew that most kids who went to stage schools kept a book of cuttings and photos from their performances.

'It's my diary and it's private,' Fay said, slipping the book into a drawer and slamming it shut.

'OK. I only asked,' Tessa murmured as she threw back her duvet and quickly got dressed.

Storm trotted invisibly at Tessa's heel as she came downstairs to the dining room. The delicious smells of eggs and bacon and toast floated towards them. Tessa asked for a big breakfast and then slipped bits of bacon and egg under the table for Storm when no one was looking.

Lessons with Judith started promptly.

Storm curled up for a nap on Tessa's lap. When a tiny rumbling snore rose from him, it was all Tessa could do to stifle her giggles.

It was history today and Tessa worked steadily, but she was glad when lessons finished for the day. 'I wonder when the director will want us,' she commented to Storm as she, Fay and Kelly tidied away their workbooks.

'Duh! When he's ready,' Kelly scoffed. 'Or maybe you think you deserve special treatment, Princess?'

Tessa flushed. She must have spoken louder than she meant to and Kelly had heard and thought she was talking to herself. She realized that she was going to have to be a lot more careful about keeping Storm a secret.

'Stop calling me "Princess"! I don't like it!' she snapped at Kelly.

'OK, Your Royal Highness,' Kelly crowed.

Chapter
THREE

'Fay Hinson, Kelly Lucas, Tessa Churchill to wardrobe and make-up, please!' a woman with a clipboard called out later that afternoon.

Judith Raunds showed them the way and they all set off eagerly.

'Yay! This is it. We're going to get our costumes and have our hair and make-up done,' Tessa whispered to

Storm as he trotted beside her.

There was a big sign that read 'Wardrobe' on one of the rooms. Inside thousands of gorgeous dresses hung in neatly labelled rows and there were countless shelves and racks of hats, gloves and shoes, and wigs on stands. Assistants fetched armfuls of Victorian clothes, complete with underwear, petticoats and black boots for the three girls.

As Tessa was helped into her costume, she noticed that her name was sewn into every item, just like a real movie star. Once the girls were dressed they went to hair and make-up. A whole hour passed before Fay, Kelly and Tessa were finished. Tessa hardly recognized herself under the curly brown wig! She

did a twirl in front of Storm so that
her skirts swung out with a silken
rustle.

Storm tucked his little rust-coloured
tail between his legs and looked up at
her with anxious midnight-blue eyes.

'What's wrong? Don't you like it?'
Tessa whispered after quickly checking
everyone was busy.

'It is a very good disguise,' Storm
woofed. 'But who is the fierce enemy
you are hiding from?'

'I'm not hiding from anyone,' Tessa
reassured him. 'I have to wear this
for the film, the same as Kelly and
Fay. We're all dressed up because
we're supposed to be three Victorian
children who find a magic watch.
We have to act in three scenes.
You'll get the idea when you see us
on set.'

'Where is on set?' Storm barked.

'It's anywhere the day's filming is
going to be. They set up lights and bits
of scenery. And the floor's marked out
so you know where to stand to say
your lines.'

Storm frowned. 'It sounds very
strange.'

Tessa smiled. 'I expect it does if you're
not used to it. Acting is really like

36

having the most brilliant game of pretend. It's just the best.'

'I like games too, especially with balls and sticks,' Storm yapped, looking much happier.

'I'll see what I can do about that later,' Tessa promised.

A young man with another clipboard appeared at the door and called for them to follow him to the rose garden at the back of the house.

Tessa let Judith, Kelly and Fay walk on ahead, so that she could talk to Storm without anyone noticing. At first the tiny puppy kept treading on her long swishing skirts and almost tumbling over his own paws.

'You'll have to walk a bit further away or you'll get swept off your feet,'

Tessa told him, trying not to laugh and
hurt his feelings.

Storm finally got the idea and padded
behind Tessa, keeping his distance.

The rose garden was surrounded by
clipped hedges. There was a pretend
stone arch and a wrought-iron seat
made of painted wood. Thick cables
trailed across the ground and there were
huge bright lights and cameras all over
the place.

Tessa noticed that Fay went and stood
all by herself. She was threading her
fingers and looking very pale and tense.
For the first time Tessa wondered if
Fay's seeming unfriendliness was really
just a bad attack of nerves.

A tall young man dressed in an old-
fashioned dark suit and a shirt with a

stiff, high collar walked through the stone arch.

'Look! That's Donny Jenton!' Tessa said excitedly.

'Wow! He's *much* better looking in real life, isn't he?' Kelly gushed.

Tessa bit back a grin. Kelly was obviously too busy being all moony-eyed over Donny to think up one of her usual mean comments!

A man got up from a canvas chair which had 'Director' on the back and started giving Donny instructions. While they were all waiting for the scene to begin, Tessa spotted a woman with a fat little dog on a lead. It had short fawn-coloured fur, bulging brown eyes and a dark muzzle and wore a collar with 'Lady' in sparkling jewels. The woman doled out doggy choc drops and Lady chomped them all up with a slobbering noise.

Storm licked his lips and gave a hopeful little woof.

Tessa smiled. 'That must be Donny's dog. The way Lady's hoovering up those treats, she'll have scoffed them all in a minute. It looks like Hollywood pooches get the star treatment too, doesn't it?' she whispered to him. 'Don't worry. You won't get left out. I'll get you a treat later.'

Everyone watched in silence as Donny's scene was filmed. He had to say his lines over and over again, while the director shouted, 'Keep rolling!' to the cameras.

The director seemed really strict. Tessa

began to feel nervous and started fidgeting about.

'Are you all right?' Storm barked worriedly.

'I'm worried about fluffing my lines,' Tessa whispered.

'I will help you,' Storm yapped eagerly.

'Thanks, but it's just stage nerves. Everyone gets them,' Tessa said, smiling.

It was sweet of Storm to offer to help. But what could he do? – after all, he was just a helpless little puppy.

An assistant came up to Tessa and handed her a gold-coloured pocket watch to hold. 'When he tells you to, the director wants you to walk over to Donny and give this to him. OK?' she asked with a kind smile.

Tessa nodded.

'How come *you* get to give Donny the watch?' Kelly complained after the assistant had left. 'I've got more lines than you. It should be me who does it!'

'Don't blame me. I'm just doing what I'm told,' Tessa said, wandering away before an argument started. It hadn't taken long for Kelly to go back to her old self.

'Your boot is undone.' Storm leapt forward and started snapping at Tessa's boot lace, which was trailing on the ground.

'Thanks, Storm, I could have tripped over that,' Tessa said, horrified by the idea of going sprawling in front of everyone.

She found a low wall to sit on and carefully placed the watch beside her before crossing one leg over the other to re-tie the boot.

To her annoyance Kelly dashed over and plonked down on the wall next to her. She really hoped Kelly wasn't going to start teasing her again. But instead Kelly smiled warmly. 'Break a leg, Tessa!' she said, which was something actors often said to each other. It meant good luck for acting in the coming scene.

'Er . . . thanks,' Tessa said, wondering why Kelly was being so friendly all of a sudden.

'See you on the set,' Kelly said abruptly. She got up and hurried away, her long skirts swishing.

Tessa frowned, puzzled. 'What was that all about?' she said to Storm.

'I do not know,' Storm woofed, but he was watching Kelly closely and his midnight-blue eyes were thoughtful.

'The director's almost ready for you. Let's move a bit closer,' Judith told Tessa. 'You'll be on first.'

Tessa's heart began to beat fast. It was a good thing she was still sitting down because her legs had turned to water. 'Oh, I need the pocket watch!' she remembered.

She reached under her skirts and felt
along the top of the wall, where she'd
placed it. But it wasn't there.

Tessa looked all around for the watch.
She checked on the other side of the
wall in case it had fallen over, but there
was no sign of it. 'It has to be here. I
only put it down a minute ago. Oh, this
is awful! The director's going to be
furious!' she cried in dismay.

Storm gazed fixedly at Kelly who was watching Tessa with a smug look on her face. His little muzzle wrinkled in a growl. 'I have an idea where it is!'

Suddenly, Tessa felt a warm tingling sensation flowing down her spine.

Something very strange was about to happen.

Chapter
FOUR

Tessa watched in utter amazement as
huge gold sparks ignited in Storm's
wavy reddish-brown fur and his ears
and tail crackled with electricity.
Raising a little front paw he sent a
burst of glittery light zooming towards
Kelly.

The light divided up into glowing
streamers which whizzed up and down

and round and round her, as if
searching for something. Then, just as if
someone had given them a signal, all
the streamers shot towards Kelly's dress
pocket and disappeared inside. No one
else seemed to have noticed anything
and Tessa realized that only she could
see Storm's magic at work.

Tessa saw Kelly's pocket bulging and

churning as if it was filled with
Mexican jumping beans.

Kelly stiffened. Her eyes widened.
'Ye-ow!' she yelled. Grabbing handfuls
of her skirts, she shook them wildly so
that her pocket tipped open and
something shiny fell out and plopped
on to the grass.

'The watch!' Tessa said, realizing all at
once how Kelly had distracted her
before pinching it off the wall.

Storm gave a triumphant little woof
and then sat down, looking pleased
with himself as every last gold sparkle
faded from his fur.

'Thanks, Storm. Clever old you!' Tessa
whispered, stroking his little head after
quickly checking that no one could see
her doing it.

Kelly stood looking warily down at the watch lying on the floor as if it might jump up and bite her. As Tessa bent down to pick it up, Kelly edged away. 'I wouldn't touch that if I were you. There's something weird about it!' she warned.

'Seems fine to me,' Tessa said, holding the watch. 'How come it was in your pocket anyway?'

'I . . . er . . . saw you drop it. And I was just coming over to give it back to you,' Kelly said.

'Yeah, right,' Tessa said, annoyed. 'That was a really mean trick to play just so I'd get into trouble. I bet you were hoping the director would ask you to give Donny the watch instead. You're just a rotten scene-stealer!'

'I'm not . . . I didn't –' Kelly shouted.

'Quiet on the set!' the director's annoyed voice interrupted. He glared at Tessa and Kelly. 'I don't need this. Someone sort it out. Now!' he shouted.

Tessa saw Judith striding towards them with a stern look on her face. 'I thought better of you two. What's going on? Out with it!' she demanded.

Kelly froze and threw Tessa a scared look. 'I . . . um. It w–was . . .' she stammered.

However angry Tessa was, she wasn't a snitch. She thought quickly. 'I couldn't find the pocket watch for our scene. And I got worried that the director would be cross. Luckily Kelly found it and she was just giving it back to me.

Sorry. I didn't mean to make so much fuss,' she apologized to Judith.

Kelly's mouth dropped open in shock. 'Um . . . Tessa's . . . right. That's exactly what happened. I'm sorry for getting angry too,' she said.

Judith looked from one to the other. She didn't seem convinced but after a moment she nodded. 'No harm's done, so we'll say no more about this. But please remember that you need to behave yourselves on the set at all times if you want to be taken seriously as actresses.'

'We will,' Tessa said.

'Definitely,' Kelly agreed. When Judith had walked away out of earshot, she grudgingly turned round to Tessa. 'You're not so bad for a spoilt rich kid, Princess.'

'Thanks for nothing!' Tessa murmured, just about managing to control her temper as Kelly walked away.

The final call for her came and Tessa just had time to flutter her fingers in a tiny wave to Storm. Then excitement took over as Tessa prepared for her first ever scene with a major Hollywood star.

'And – action!'

Despite her nerves, Tessa remembered

her lines perfectly. When she stood on the right mark and gave the watch to Donny he winked at her encouragingly. Time seemed to fly and then she had to pretend to be shy and run away.

'And − cut!'

'Thank you, Tessa. Good job,' the director said. He turned to Kelly and Fay and waved to them to come on to the set.

Tessa sat on a chair with Storm on her lap, watching Fay and Kelly act. They were both good but Tessa had goose pimples while Fay was speaking. It was obvious to everyone that the shy girl had something special.

'She just lights up when she's acting,' Tessa said, stroking Storm's silky head. 'I wish I was that good.'

'You are. You just don't see it in yourself,' Storm woofed loyally.

'OK, we're done for now.' The director glanced towards Judith. 'I'll need all the girls back on Thursday afternoon.'

Tessa felt a bit disappointed. Thursday was two whole days away.

Judith smiled as she led them back to wardrobe and make-up. 'Well done. This director doesn't say very much, but I could tell that he was delighted with all of you.'

Later that day when Tessa and Storm were alone, Tessa gave the little puppy a big hug. 'And you were brilliant today too, Storm. I didn't know you could do magic like that! Thanks for getting the gold watch back from Kelly.'

'You are welcome,' Storm barked happily.

After supper, Tessa took Storm for a walk in the grounds. He rushed around, ears flapping, as he investigated the flower beds and sniffed around the trees.

Back in the big house, Tessa phoned her mum and dad.

They were delighted to hear all about the scene she had acted in with Donny. 'And how about the other girls? Are they nice? Have you made friends with them?' Mrs Churchill asked at the end of the conversation.

'I have made one brilliant new friend,' Tessa said, beaming at Storm.

Tessa said her goodbyes and went up to her room. Storm scampered eagerly upstairs beside her.

Fay was sitting on her bed in a pool of light from her reading lamp. She wore a pair of yellow pyjamas with pink teddies and had her diary open on her lap. 'Where's Kelly?' she asked Tessa.

Tessa shrugged. 'I don't know. Maybe she's in the sitting room. Judith and some other people are in there watching a film on TV. It was great today, wasn't it? I really love acting.'

Fay smiled shyly and her hazel eyes sparkled. 'Me too. It wasn't half as bad as I'd expected. I was really dreading it.'

'But you were really good. Everyone

thought so,' Tessa said, surprised. Fay had said her lines perfectly and she'd only had to do them once before the director was satisfied.

'Do you think so?' Fay asked anxiously. 'I always try so hard, but I never think I'm good enough.'

'My dad says that you can't do any more than your best,' Tessa told her. 'That's what I think of when I get stage fright.'

'I'll remember that. Thanks,' Fay said. She got into bed and slipped her diary into her bedside drawer before turning off the lamp. 'Night. See you in the morning, Tessa.'

'Night, Fay.'

Storm leapt on to Tessa's bed and turned round in circles, making himself a soft nest in the duvet. As Tessa got undressed, she smiled to herself. Perhaps she might leave Harpford Manor with more than one new friend after all.

Chapter
FIVE

After lessons the following morning,
Judith drove Fay, Kelly and Tessa,
with Storm invisibly snuggled up on
her lap, into the nearest big town. 'I
thought we deserved a treat, and as
you're not needed until tomorrow we
have plenty of spare time,' she told
them.

'I wonder where we're going,' Fay

said to Tessa, as Judith looked for
somewhere to park.

'We'll find out in a minute, won't
we?' Kelly mocked. 'How come you
and Princess are suddenly all buddy-
buddy, anyway?'

'We're not!' Tessa snapped without
thinking and then she noticed Fay's
hurt look. 'I mean, we are kind of . . .

And if you don't stop calling me
"Princess" . . . I won't be responsible!'

'Huh! Who's dented your crown?'
Kelly drawled.

'Look!' Fay called hurriedly as they
passed a cinema. 'Donny Jenton's latest
film is on.'

'I know,' Judith said, grinning. 'That's
where we're going.'

The film was great. It was all about
thieves who are trying to steal a rich
prince's fortune, and had loads of special
effects. Meera Brook, a gorgeous young
actress, was starring with Donny. She
had long dark hair and a tiny waist and
wore fabulous silk gowns.

They all watched the cinema screen
spellbound.

Storm was a bit scared of the loud

noises and flashing lights at first but he soon settled down and enjoyed the film when he realized there was no danger. 'See, Storm, it's all just pretend,' Tessa said soothingly.

Storm took the film very seriously. He growled when Donny's carriage was attacked and woofed excitedly when Donny rescued Meera from a horrible bandit with a bristling beard who was slashing about with a curved sword.

'Oooh, Donny looks mega-lush!' Kelly enthused with a soppy look on her face. 'I wish I was Meera Brook.'

After the film ended, Judith took them all for a pizza. Tessa got

permission to pop into the superstore
which was two doors down. She went
straight to the pet department and
bought a small bag of choc drops and a
dog chew.

Once they all got back to Harpford
Manor, Tessa found a quiet spot in the
grounds to give Storm his treats.

'These taste good,' he woofed, licking
his chops.

'Well, I don't see why Lady should be
the only pampered dog around here!'
Tessa said. 'But if you eat too many
you'll soon be a little porker!'

Storm polished off the dog chew too
and then flopped on to the grass and
rolled on to his back with his tongue
lolling out. Tessa smiled as she rubbed
his fat rust-coloured tummy. She felt a
surge of affection for the gorgeous little
pup. 'I wish you could stay with me
forever. When I become a famous
actress, you can travel everywhere with
me.'

Storm rolled on to his front and then
stood up and shook himself. 'That is
not possible. One day I must return to

my own world and lead the Moon-claw
pack. Do you understand that, Tessa?' he
asked, his midnight-blue eyes wide and
serious.

Tessa nodded sadly, but she didn't
want to think about that now. She
decided to change the subject instead.
'How do you fancy a long walk before
I phone Mum and Dad?'

'My favourite thing!' Storm woofed,
eagerly wagging his tail.

They went down tree-lined paths
and past clipped hedges until they
came to a gate leading to an open
field with a river at the bottom.
Colourful wild flowers nodded in the
grass and there was a footpath that
seemed to lead to a village in the
distance.

Storm lifted his head, his little brown nose twitching. Suddenly, he shot forward like a rocket. 'Rabbits!' he yapped happily.

Tessa smiled as Storm zigzagged after the rabbits, his short, sturdy legs going like pistons. They scattered in all directions and shot down their rabbit holes. Storm didn't seem to mind that they all avoided him easily. He was content with snapping at disappearing white cottontails.

After half an hour, Storm lolloped over to Tessa, panting heavily, with his floppy ears flying out behind him.

Tessa bent down to pat him. 'You look worn out. I bet you're thirsty after all that tearing about. Let's go back and you can have a drink in our bathroom. It'll be quieter than the kitchen and no one will notice what we're doing.'

As they drew near to the main house, Tessa saw Fay sitting on a bench, reading *The Stage* newspaper in a patch of late afternoon sunlight. Tessa waved to her and Fay waved back.

Tessa and Storm went inside the manor house and made their way straight upstairs. As she approached their room, Tessa heard someone chuckling. 'That sounds like Kelly. What's she up to?'

'I do not know,' Storm yapped suspiciously.

Tessa saw that the older girl was lying on her bed on her tummy. She was reading a thick book with a familiar green cover. 'That's Fay's diary! You shouldn't be reading it!' Tessa exclaimed.

Kelly looked up and started guiltily. 'Oh, it's only you,' she said.

'Put it back in the drawer right now!' Tessa demanded.

'Or what,' Kelly sneered. 'I've got a right to read stuff she's written about me, haven't I? I know she's jealous of me because I've got lots more lines to say and Donny likes me better than you or Fay, I can tell.'

Tessa lunged forward and tried to grab the diary, but Kelly held it out of her reach. 'Stop reading it. It's private,' Tessa said, kneeling on the bed.

Kelly ignored her. 'Listen to this,' she began, reading aloud. '"It's hard to keep up with the others. I always take ages to learn my lines. Everyone else seems to know what to do, but I have to keep asking. They're all better than me at acting."' She sniggered. 'How wet is that?'

'Give me that diary,' Tessa said through clenched teeth.

Kelly sat up. 'Have the stupid thing. It's boring anyway. She hasn't written a single word about me. Catch!' she said, throwing the diary across the room.

It crashed to the floor with a thud and landed heavily on one corner. The cover buckled and twisted and some pages fell out.

'Oops!' Kelly said. 'I'm off. See you!'

She ran out and Tessa heard steps hurrying down the stairs.

Tessa bent down to pick up the diary. 'Look at the state of it now! Fay's going to be so upset.'

'I will help you to mend it,' Storm offered.

Tessa felt another warm tingling feeling trickle down her spine as Storm's rusty-coloured fur lit up with bright gold sparks and his floppy ears glittered with power. A fountain of golden light arched towards the book in Tessa's hands.

Tiny gold sparks like busy worker bees zizzed all over the diary, which squirmed in Tessa's hands as Storm's magic went to work.

Suddenly, footsteps sounded again on

the stairs. 'Tessa, are you in there?' called a voice. 'They've got table tennis. Do you fancy a game?'

'Oh, no! It's Fay!' Tessa whispered desperately.

Chapter
SIX

The sparks in Storm's fur instantly went out. Tessa looked down at the diary. It looked worse than before. The cover was all lumps and bumps, one corner was badly dented and even more pages were hanging out.

'I did not have time to finish my magic with Fay so close,' Storm woofed apologetically.

Tessa quickly put the diary behind
her back as Fay walked in.

'Hi. I've been looking for —' Fay
broke off, looking puzzled, and her
smile faded. 'What have you got behind
your back?'

Tessa gulped. She knew that Fay
would be deeply upset if she found out
that Kelly had been reading her private
thoughts. She slowly brought her hands
forward. 'I . . . um . . . just came in and
found this lying on the bed. I was
going to put it back in your drawer, but
I dropped it and the cover got a bit
bashed. Sorry,' she finished lamely.

Fay frowned. 'I *never* leave my diary
on my bed.'

'Perhaps you forgot this time?' Tessa
suggested.

Fay's face darkened. 'No, I didn't.
You've been reading it, haven't you?' she
said in a wavery voice. 'Don't try and
pretend you haven't. I bet you thought
my scribbles were so pathetic that you
kicked my poor diary all round the
room and then jumped on it or
something!'

'I didn't. I wouldn't ever do that!'
Tessa exclaimed.

'Looks like it, doesn't it?' Fay snatched
her diary and then stood there hugging
it to her chest and stroking it. 'I
thought you liked me, but you were
only pretending. I thought you were
different, Tessa.'

Tessa felt terrible, even though none of
this was her fault. She knew that Fay
wouldn't believe anything she said now,
but she still had to try. 'I *do* like you, Fay.
And I didn't read your diary. Honest.
Cross my heart and hope to die!'

But Fay wasn't listening any more.
She threw herself on to her bed, buried
her face in her pillow and curled up
with both arms wrapped round the
diary.

Sighing heavily, Tessa trudged towards
the bathroom.

Storm padded in after her and she closed the door behind him. 'I am sorry. I have made things worse,' he woofed sadly.

Tessa stroked his silky head. 'You were only trying to help. Besides, this is all Kelly's fault.'

Tessa emptied a soap dish and washed it out before pouring water into it for Storm. 'And just when I thought I was starting to get on better with Fay,' she murmured as she watched the tiny puppy lapping thirstily.

The following day it was lessons again and then hours spent in costume and make-up before filming another scene with Donny. This time it was inside Harpford Manor's great hall.

It was a long scene and Tessa had a
lot of lines to say. The director was very
demanding and bossed everyone about
but seemed satisfied with the way
things went.

When he called for a coffee break,
Tessa decided that she'd go and sit
with Fay to have another go at trying
to put things right. She passed Kelly,
who was sitting munching a bag of
crisps.

'I wouldn't bother looking for Fay if
I were you,' Kelly said. 'She's gone off
somewhere by herself. I bet she's
writing more stuff in her soppy old
diary.'

'Get knotted, Kelly!' Tessa said crossly,
having to make a huge effort not to say
something even worse. 'Grrr. Why does

that girl have to be so mean?' she
complained to Storm.

There wasn't time to go searching for
Fay, so Tessa fetched a cold drink and
then sat down with Storm. 'Fay
probably hates me now. I bet she'll

never speak to me again,' she said to him.

'I do not think that anyone could hate you,' Storm woofed, patting her leg with one soft little rusty paw.

'Thanks, Storm.' As Tessa reached down and took hold of the loyal pup's paw, she felt herself starting to calm down. An idea popped into her head. 'Why don't we walk across the field to the village later? Maybe it will have a shop that sells diaries. I can buy Fay a new one!'

Storm nodded. 'I think Fay would like that.'

'She'll probably think I'm just trying to make up with her because I've got a guilty conscience,' Tessa guessed. 'But at least it might make her feel a bit better.'

'You have a very kind heart, Tessa,'
Storm yapped, wagging his tail.

'Try telling Fay that!' Tessa sighed.

The call came for filming to
begin again and the actors began
moving towards the set. Tessa gave
Storm a quick pat and went back to

work, feeling a little better about everything.

'I was proud of you all today,' Judith said to them later as they all ate supper together. 'The director was even more demanding than usual. But you just did as he asked.'

Tessa was feeling really full. She'd asked for another big meal, so that she could share it with Storm. But it was difficult to slip food under the table to him, with everyone talking to her, and she'd had to eat most of it herself.

'I wish we got to see more of Donny,' Kelly commented wistfully. 'I'm his number-one fan, but I haven't even had a chance to ask him for his autograph.'

'He's known to be quite a private person when he's not working,' Judith said.

Fay was picking at her baked potato and salad. After only eating a little, she asked to be excused and left the table.

'Is Fay all right?' Judith asked. 'She's very quiet.'

'She's always like that,' Kelly piped up. 'She's probably just trying to seem interesting and mysterious, like Donny.'

'I think she's still upset because her diary got damaged,' Tessa said, giving Kelly a hard look. She was pleased to see that Kelly looked a tiny bit shamefaced.

'What's that about a diary?' Judith said.

'Oh, the cover got a bit bent, but it's nothing really,' Kelly said. She lowered her voice. 'Some people can't take a joke.'

Tessa stood up before she said something very rude indeed. She wanted to walk over to the village. 'I think I'll go and get some exercise,' she said to Judith as she left the table. 'But first I'll get some ham sandwiches for a snack later.' *At least Storm will have some supper*, she thought.

'Goodness me. Where do you put it all?' Judith said, smiling.

'I've always had a big appetite,' Tessa said hastily, making for the counter.

She took her wrapped package and headed outside with Storm. He scampered after her, his nose twitching at the smell of the ham sandwiches. Once they were by themselves, Tessa broke them into small pieces for him.

Storm chomped them up and then licked his chops. 'Delicious!'

'Ready for an extra-long walk now? As if I need to ask!' Tessa said, grinning.

As they headed towards Harpford

Manor's main gates, they saw some film
equipment stacked up to one side
beside the path. Leaning against it were
some wooden boards painted with
scenery.

Suddenly, a podgy little fawn-coloured
dog with a sparkling collar and a
trailing lead shot through the gateway.
It was Lady!

'She must have run off! Lady! Come
here,' Tessa called in a friendly, gentle
way. But the pug shied away and ran
sideways.

'I will catch her,' Storm yapped
helpfully, bounding forward.

Lady ran headlong towards the
scenery brushing against it as she
looked for a hiding place in this
exciting new game. One of the big

lights that sat right on the top of the stack of film equipment wobbled. It was going to fall!

Tessa looked on in horror as it began to topple towards the ground – with Storm right beneath it!

Chapter
SEVEN

'Look out!' Tessa shouted.

Storm was too intent on snapping at Lady's trailing lead to notice the danger. Tessa realized that he wouldn't have time to use his magical powers.

Without a second thought she threw herself forward. One step, two steps. Scoop! Scoop! By a complete miracle she managed to grab both Storm and

Lady by the scruff of their necks. With
a dog in each hand, she hurtled to one
side as the heavy light crashed down,
missing them all by centimetres.

Tessa stumbled and slipped, twisting
her ankle. 'Oh,' she gasped as a sharp
pain shot through her leg.

Somehow she managed to keep hold

of the two dogs as she collapsed on to the soft grass.

'Thank you for saving me,' Storm woofed, looking subdued as she set him on his feet. 'You were very brave.'

'I'm not really. I couldn't bear anything to happen to you,' Tessa said. She put Lady down too, but kept a firm hold on the pug's lead. As the ache in her ankle increased, she winced.

'You are hurt. I will make you better,' Storm woofed.

Just then Tessa saw a tall figure walking towards the gateway. It was Donny Jenton, completely alone and without his security guards. 'There isn't time. Donny's almost here!' she hissed at Storm.

A familiar warm tingling sensation

flowed down Tessa's spine, but this time there was a rush of backwards movement, just as if she had pressed rewind on her DVD player.

Storm's bright eyes narrowed in concentration as he huffed out a warm puppy breath of tiny gold sparkles. The glittering mist gently swirled round Tessa's sore ankle, sank into it, and she felt the pain fade away completely. There was a sudden jerking movement and Tessa was flicked forward again. She saw that Donny was still the same distance away – no time at all had actually passed!

'Thanks, Storm. That was brilliant. I'm fine now,' she whispered.

'Gruff! Gruff!' Lady barked, trying to wriggle free.

Donny reached out for his dog's lead. 'You're Tessa, aren't you?' he said, his white teeth gleaming as he smiled. 'I saw what you just did. How can I ever thank you for saving Lady?'

'It's no big deal. It just sort of . . . happened,' Tessa said, going red.

'Well, you were very brave. Maybe a little dumb too, to risk getting squashed

by that heavy light. I don't think your parents would approve. But don't worry, I won't tell anyone,' Donny said with a twinkle in his eye.

He gave Lady a cuddle. 'Bad girl. Why did you take off like that?' he scolded, wagging his finger as Lady snuffled and licked his nose.

'Maybe she wanted a good long run off her lead,' Tessa suggested. 'She probably gets bored just sitting around and being fed treats. And I hope you don't mind me saying, but she's a bit overweight.'

Donny raised his eyebrows. 'Really? Why hasn't anyone else told me that?'

Tessa wisely decided not to answer.

Donny put Lady down on the floor.

'Let's get you back. From now on, you're going to get a lot *more* exercise and the choccy drops are history!' He looked at Tessa. 'Thanks again, honey. Can I give you a lift back up the drive to the front door? My driver's parked just down the road.'

'Thanks, but I've got some shopping to do. I think I'm still going to go into the village,' Tessa said.

'Well, OK. Isn't there anything I can do for you? I'd like to show my appreciation for the way you saved Lady,' Donny said.

'No, I don't think . . .' Tessa paused as an idea jumped into her mind. 'Well, maybe there is something . . .'

Donny listened as Tessa explained her idea and then he grinned. 'I'd be

delighted. How about after filming
finishes tomorrow? My driver will pick
you up.' He gave Tessa a quick wave as
he set off with Lady puffing noisily
beside him.

As Tessa had hoped, there was a
newsagent's shop in the village.

She did her shopping and then decided
to return to Harpford Manor along
the footpath that ran across the field.
Storm trotted at Tessa's heel, his nose
to the ground as he snuffled about.
The trip had been a success and Tessa
now carried a bag containing a brand-
new diary, covered in shiny green
plastic. It even had a strap with a heart-
shaped padlock and a key to lock it
with.

'I really hope this cheers Fay up –
even just a little bit,' she said, glancing
down at Storm.

But he seemed to have run off.

'Storm? Where are you?' Tessa
called.

She looked across the field, expecting
to see him chasing rabbits, but there

was no sign of him. Puzzled, she circled round, scanning the field more carefully, and just spotted the tip of Storm's rusty-coloured tail as he dived into the bottom of a hedgerow.

She hurried over. 'What's this hide and seek –' she began and then stopped as she realized that Storm was trembling all over. She bent down and looked through the tangled branches at him. 'What's wrong?'

'Shadow has found me! He has put a spell on those dogs!' Storm whined in terror, his midnight-blue eyes wide and fearful.

'What dogs, Storm?' Tessa looked up. In the next field a man with two black-and-white sheepdogs was herding some sheep into a pen. The dogs

were running back and forth and
snapping at the sheep's heels.

'I don't *think* those dogs are after you.
But how can I tell if they're under a
magic spell?' Tessa asked Storm.

Storm whimpered and burrowed
deeper into the hedgerow. 'They
will have pale cold eyes and extra-
long teeth. And be very fierce and
strong.'

Tessa looked hard at the sheepdogs, which were following their owner's orders closely. 'They don't look like that. I think they're OK. But you've had a nasty fright. Let's get back,' Tessa said.

Storm squirmed towards her and she bent down and reached for the terrified puppy. As Tessa set off again with Storm in her arms, she felt his little heart fluttering against her hand. The glimpse of possible danger reminded Tessa again that Storm might have to leave suddenly in order to save himself.

She felt a pang as she realized that however much she might try to prepare herself for losing Storm she would never be ready to let him go.

Chapter
EIGHT

The moment Tessa and Storm reached Harpford Manor, they set off to find Fay and give her the new diary. Tessa checked the sitting room and the games room before she finally tracked her down in their bedroom.

Fay was reading a book. She looked up as Tessa came in and gave her a small smile.

Tessa felt encouraged. At least Fay seemed willing to talk. 'Good book?' she asked hopefully.

Fay nodded. 'It's fairy stories, with really great illustrations. See? Ogres, goblins and monsters, and there's a handsome prince who rescues a beautiful princess from a swamp monster.'

'Sounds exciting,' Tessa said, even though she didn't think she'd fancy reading it herself. She went and peered over Fay's shoulder. 'The prince looks a bit like Donny. Don't show it to Kelly or she'll get drool all over the page!'

Fay giggled. 'Tessa. I wanted to talk to –' she began shyly.

'OK, but me first,' Tessa said quickly,

thrusting the plastic bag at Fay. 'I got
you this. I hope you like it.'

'For me?' Fay's eyes widened as she
reached inside the bag and took out
the shiny new diary. 'Oh, it's brilliant!
And it locks too. Look at this cute little
key.'

'Yes. So no one can read your diary
now,' Tessa said. 'Look, about the other
evening. I know you probably still
won't believe that I didn't read −'

'But I do believe you!' Fay broke in excitedly. 'That's what I was about to tell you just now. I came in here and caught Kelly reading my diary earlier and she admitted everything. She couldn't even be bothered to lie. Anyway, I know that you had nothing to do with what happened.'

Tessa took a second or two to let this sink in. 'Good. So . . . um . . . we can be friends now?'

'If you still want to,' Fay said, her hazel eyes sparkling. 'And thanks loads for my new diary. I love it to bits.'

'You're welcome,' Tessa said, beaming. 'And guess who I just saw on the way to the village when I went to buy it. Donny Jenton!'

'Really? Did he have heaps of

bodyguards with him?' Fay asked.

'No. He was all by himself. He
was looking for Lady, who'd escaped
and run away.' Tessa told Fay about
dashing after Lady and almost getting
flattened by the heavy light but she
missed out all mention of Storm.
'Donny was so pleased that Lady was
safe that he offered me a reward. At first
I couldn't think of anything I wanted.
But then I asked if he'd take me and
my friends out for a burger or
something.'

'You didn't!' Fay said, deeply
impressed. 'What did he say?'

Tessa smiled. 'He was dead keen. He's
arranging for his car to pick us up after
we finish filming tomorrow.'

'Wow! That's so cool!' Fay exclaimed.

'Wait until Kelly hears about this!'

'Hears about what?' Kelly demanded from the open doorway. 'As if I'd be interested in any of your pathetic plans!'

'So you don't want to hear about how Fay and me are going out for a burger with Donny tomorrow evening?' Tessa said casually.

'What? Don't make me laugh!' Kelly said. 'Soppy old Fay and silly, spoilt Princess going on a date with Donny? As if!'

Tessa kept hold of her temper. She shrugged. 'Well, you'll see for yourself, won't you? When Donny sends his car for us.'

'Yeah, right!' Kelly crowed, but she didn't look so sure of herself now. 'Why

would he want to take you two
muppets anywhere?'

'Because Tessa saved Lady from
getting squashed when some equipment
almost fell on her,' Fay said. 'Isn't that
right, Tessa?'

Tessa nodded. 'Donny's *my* number-
one fan now. I might get his autograph
for you, if you ask me really, really

nicely!' she teased Kelly and was pleased to see the older girl flush with jealousy. She turned to Fay. 'Fancy a game of table tennis?'

'You bet!' Fay cried, linking arms with Tessa. They swanned past Kelly with Storm trotting invisibly after them.

'I don't believe a word of it. You're just a zonking great fibber, Tessa Churchill!' Kelly shouted after them.

'Am I? We'll see,' Tessa replied smugly.

Halfway down the stairs Tessa and Fay clapped their hands over their mouths and started to laugh. 'Did you see the look on her face? You are *so* bad!' Fay whispered through her fingers.

'I couldn't help it!' Tessa answered. 'I really enjoyed getting my own back for once. Besides, Kelly won't be left out

for long. I'll tell her tomorrow that
she's invited to come with us!'

Tessa held up her long skirts as she
emerged from wardrobe in full costume
the following morning. 'I can't believe
that this is my last day of filming. It's
gone by so fast!' she whispered to Storm.

Storm nodded, his midnight-blue eyes
looking a little troubled.

'Are you looking forward to coming
home with me? Mum and Dad are
going to love you,' Tessa said.

But Storm didn't answer. She noticed
that he kept glancing nervously around
as he followed Tessa down to the big
old-fashioned kitchen where the scene
was being filmed. 'Is something wrong?'
she asked him.

'Shadow is very close now. I can feel it. He will use his magic to make any dogs nearby hunt me down,' the terrified puppy whined, beginning to tremble like a leaf.

'Oh, no!' Tessa gasped, going cold all over. 'Maybe it's another false alarm.'

Storm shook his head. 'Not this time.'

Tessa racked her brains, trying to think of what to do. 'I know! How about hiding among the costumes? There are thousands of them. It would be hard for any dogs to find you in there. As soon as I've finished this scene, I'll come and fetch you.'

'It is a good plan,' Storm agreed. He set off, ears and tail flying.

Somehow Tessa followed the director's instructions and remembered all her lines. The second she was free, she hared off towards wardrobe.

As Tessa reached it, Storm shot towards her in terror, ducking into a side room. There were three mongrel dogs hard on his heels. They had pale eyes and extra-long teeth and were growling fiercely.

Tessa's heart missed a beat. Her plan hadn't worked! Storm was in terrible danger.

She rushed after the tiny puppy and fierce enemy dogs just as a dazzling flash of gold light stopped her in her tracks. When the light faded, Tessa rubbed the sparkles from her eyes to see that Storm stood there, a helpless puppy no longer, but his true magnificent wolf self. An older female wolf with a gentle face stood next to him.

Tessa realized that the moment she had been dreading was here. She was going to have to be very brave. 'Go! Save yourself, Storm!' she cried, her voice breaking.

Storm's midnight-blue eyes shone

with affection, and gold dust glimmered in his thick silver-grey neck-ruff. 'Be of good heart, Tessa. You have been a true friend,' he said in a velvety growl.

There was a final bright gold flash and Storm and his mother began to fade before disappearing forever. The mongrel dogs leapt forward, but they were too late. Their eyes and teeth instantly returned to normal and they slunk out.

Tessa gulped. It had all happened so fast. She felt stunned. 'I'll never forget you, Storm,' she whispered as tears pricked her eyes.

Tessa had just finished drying her eyes when Fay popped her head into the room. 'I've been looking for you. It's almost five thirty. We have to get out of these costumes before we go and meet Donny. I've just told Kelly that we're *all* going for a burger. You should have seen her face!'

'I bet it was priceless,' Tessa said, smiling despite herself.

As she went with Fay, Tessa felt herself beginning to get excited again at the thought of meeting up with Donny Jenton – she knew so many people who would give anything to be in her place.

But whatever the future held, Tessa knew that her secret magic puppy friend, Storm, would always be the true star of her life.

Magic Puppy

Win a Magic Puppy goody bag!

The evil wolf Shadow has ripped out part of Storm's letter from his mother and hidden the words so that magic puppy Storm can't find them.

Storm needs your help!

Four words have been hidden in secret bones in the first four Magic Puppy books. Find the hidden words and put them together to complete the message from Storm's mother. Send it in to us and each month we will put every correct message in a draw and pick out one lucky winner, who will receive a Magic Puppy gift – definitely worth barking about!

Send the hidden message, your name and address on a postcard to:

Magic Puppy Competition

Puffin Books

80 Strand

London WC2R 0RL

Good luck!

Magic Puppy

A New Beginning
9780141323503

Muddy Paws
9780141323510

Cloud Capers
9780141323527

Star of the Show
9780141323534

puffin.co.uk